Rumpelstiltskin

Story written by Karra McFarlane
Illustrated by Fabio Mancini

How to help your child read this book

This book gives your child extra practice in reading a story that includes sounds he or she has learnt at school.

Ask your child to read the Story Green Words and Red Words below, before reading the story. Do not read the story to your child first. Point to the words as he or she reads. If your child hesitates, help him or her to sound-blend the word.

Re-read each sentence or page to keep the plot moving. Children's attention is focused on reading the words and they find it hard to focus on the story at the same time.

Don't make them struggle too much and praise them when they succeed. Do it all with patience and love!

Story Green Words

Story Green Words are made up of sounds your child has already learnt. This book contains the following green words:

necklace incredibly adorable Rumpelstiltskin

uncontrollable castle Belle

Red Words

Red Words are harder to read because the letters represent unusual sounds. Ask your child to read the red words, but if he or she gets stuck on a word, read the word to your child. This book contains the following red words:

wanted who could thought

what's one

Important note

Read stories to your children that are beyond the level they can read for themselves – every evening. They'll only want to become readers if they experience the joy of listening to a range of stories, non-fiction and poetry. Very soon, they will be able to read those books for themselves, as well as listen to them.

Vocabulary check

Tell your child the meaning of each word in the context of the story.

	definition:	sentence:
miller	someone who grinds corn or wheat to make flour	A poor miller wanted to impress the king.
remarkable	deserving attention	So he told the king that he had a remarkable child …
unbelievable	cannot be believed	The king thought this was unbelievable.
appeared	came into view	… a little man appeared in the room.
announced	delivered the news	"I know how to do it," the little man announced.
finest	very best	… he spun the straw into the finest gold.
first-born	the first child that a mother gives birth to	"… you must give me your first-born child," …
incredibly	very or extremely	… the king was incredibly pleased.
uncontrollably	without being able to stop	Belle sobbed uncontrollably.
messenger	a person who carries information to someone	… Belle's messenger told her that he had seen a strange little man …

A poor miller wanted to impress the king. So he told the king that he had a remarkable child, Belle, who could spin straw into gold.

The king thought this was unbelievable. "Bring her to me!" he commanded.

The king put Belle in a room filled with straw.

"Spin this straw into gold before morning," he ordered.

Belle did not know how. She began to weep.

Suddenly, a little man appeared in the room.
"What's wrong?" he asked.

Belle told him her story.

"I know how to do it," the little man announced. "But, first, give me your necklace."

Belle gave him her necklace, and he spun the straw into the finest gold.

The next morning, the king was delighted with the gold. But he wanted more.
He put Belle in a room filled with even more straw and told her to spin it into gold by morning.

That night, the little man came back, but Belle had nothing else to give him.

"If I spin this straw into gold, you must give me your first-born child," the little man said.

Thinking that it was unbelievable that she might ever have a child, Belle agreed.

The next morning, the king was incredibly pleased.

Soon after, the king and Belle wed and she became queen. They had an adorable child together.

Then, one night, the little man came back. He demanded that Belle hand over her child. Belle sobbed uncontrollably.

"If you can guess my name in three days," the horrible man whispered, "you can keep your child."

Each day, the man came back, and, each day, Belle tried to guess his name.

Then, on the third day, Belle's messenger told her that he had seen a strange little man in the forest, singing a song:

"Oh, it's such a shame,
Queen Belle will never know my name,
This is a game I am sure to win,
She will never guess it's Rumpelstiltskin!"

That night, the man came back and Belle guessed his name correctly. "Is it Rumpelstiltskin?" she asked.

The little man was furious! He jumped up and down in an uncontrollable rage.

But as he had promised, Belle kept her child and they lived happily in the king's castle.

Questions to read and answer

Ask your child to read the questions and answer them without your help.

1. Why did the miller lie to the king?

2. How did the king feel when he saw all the gold?

3. What did Rumpelstiltskin do with the straw?

4. Why doesn't Rumpelstiltskin think Belle will guess his name?

5. Why did Rumpelstiltskin let Belle keep her child?

Retell the story

Take turns retelling the story with your child.